THIS BOOK BELONGS TO:

First published in Great Britain in 2016 by Hodder and Stoughton
Copyright © Mo Farah Limited, 2016

A CIP catalogue record of this book is available from
the British Library.

ISBN 978 1 444 93407 6

10 9 8 7 6 5 4 3

Hodder Children's Books
An imprint of Hachette Children's Group
Part of Hodder and Stoughton
Carmelite House
50 Victoria Embankment
London EC4Y 0DZ

Printed and bound in Europe

An Hachette UK Company
www.hachettechildrens.co.uk

READY STEADY MO!

Mo Farah
Kes Gray and Marta Kissi

Hodder
Children's
Books

YO!
I'm little
MO.

Where do you live?
And where do you go?

How do you get there?

Does it feel fun?

Here's what I'm thinking.
Why don't you. . .

RUN

Run to the kitchen,
Run to the sink,

Run for a sandwich,

Run for a drink.

Run round the table,
Run round the chairs,
Run down the hallway,

Run up the stairs.

Run in your slippers,

Run in your vest,

Run in your onesie,

Run and get dressed.

Run round
the garden,

Run round the park,

Run in the daylight,

Run
in
the
dark.

Run on the pavement,
Run on the grass,
Run in the playground,

Perhaps not in class.

Run with a football,
Run with a kite,

Run to the left,

Run to the right.

Run in a straight line,

Run round some bends,

Run round

Run with your family,
Run with your friends.

Run in the country,
Run in the town,

Run going up, Run going down.

Run with a cheetah,
Run with a snail,
Run with a dolphin,
Run with a whale.

Run in a fun run,
Run in a race,

Pop on a space suit,

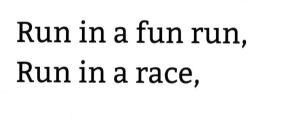

AND
RUN
INTO
SPACE!

Run round the universe,
Run on the spot,

Run
out
of
puff…

. . .and do the MOBOT!